LIGHTNIN

Jeri Chase-Ferris, author of *Noah Webster & His Words,* published by Houghton Mifflin Harcourt, a 2012 Junior Library Guild fall selection and winner of the 2013 Golden Kite Award for children's non-fiction says: "*Lightning Strikes* is filled with really beautiful word pictures and wonderful descriptions of life in a small and innocent town . . . an exquisite, evocative story from a simpler, though not completely rose-colored era, captured in a young boy's eyes."

Lonon Smith, Hollywood screenwriter, director, and author of *Wise Men,* says, "I liked the story a lot. It has a wonderful feel of the heat and rain and smell of small town midwest America, and an interesting arc that goes where I didn't expect, a plus. It's good work."

Robert Pacholik, author of *Night Flares,* a Vietnam short-story collection, says, "*Lightning Strikes* is about a child's innocence stretched to the limit by the deeds of his family, his visions of wrong, and what is right . . . highly recommended."

Lightning Strikes

Daniel Babka

Blue Squirrel Press
Roseville, California

ISBN (paperback): 978-0-9910601-3-9
ISBN (ebook): 978-0-9910601-0-8

Library of Congress Control Number: 2014904141

First Edition: July 2014 by Blue Squirrel Press, Roseville, CA

Cover Photo by Ben Thompson Photography
flickr.com/photos/benft/

Interior Production by Williams Writing, Editing & Design
www.williamswriting.com

For my mother, Lois,
who has given so much to all her children,
to my grandfather and to Wally.
And to my daughter, Shannon, and Delilah
Renn – so you'll know something more.

ACKNOWLEDGMENTS

"Lightning Strikes"........................special thanks to Cindy Riley-Burch for her constant support and to Nick Overocker, friend, former Marine, and hard-driving editor extraordinaire who wouldn't accept anything less than the best I was capable of. You made the difference. Thank you for your help in bringing the story to life.

LIGHTNING STRIKES

The Heights is where all the black people lived in Twinsburg, Ohio, in the late fifties. The adults I knew called it the colored settlement. My father and grandfather ran whiskey and beer up there and took me with them. It wasn't the kind of bootlegging Robert Mitchum did in the movie, Thunder Road, when he ran moonshine in a two-door, '51 Ford. What we did seemed ordinary. Just the same, I don't remember anybody getting arrested for anything serious before that night.

Grandpa George and I would carry the cases up the basement stairs, look sideways at the police station next door, load up the trunk, and stack the boxes on the Packard's backseat. I was twelve, but I still got to sit on top of the whiskey when he drove up the hill.

My grandpa and dad both told me it wasn't just for the money. They said they took the risks because everybody had a right to drink, and no one else was willing to sell to the colored joints in The Heights that couldn't get a liquor license.

Most white folks never went there, except to pick up the help. Me, I spent a lot of time with my friend Ike, and his twin sister Ada, and some other kids. So I knew my way around. The people who lived in The Heights sat on porches, hung their clothes out to dry, and grew sunflowers in their yards just like the people in town. They had less stuff, but I didn't see as how anybody was that different.

The roads on the hill were dirt and cinder, except for the paved one that marked the east-west border and cut through to a county road on the other side of the settlement, the one Craig Dodson's mom drove us down in her '56 Woody to see Tarzan movies for a quarter. The fact that Ike and my other black friends didn't ever have an extra quarter never occurred to me, in the same way I never noticed how Grandpa George gave me a three-speed English racer for my birthday and only gave my two sisters a box of crayons to share.

We spent our days riding bikes, and playing sports and games like Kick the Can and Three Feet in the Mud Gutter. Ike used to come over for lunch sometimes. Isiah was his long name but everybody called him Ike, like the president. He got spaghetti sauce on his shirt once and I gave him one of mine to wear. He could hardly get over that. There were a lot of colored kids like Ike and Ada, who didn't have much besides one or two changes of clothes and what they had on. I didn't understand or pay much attention to it then, but I knew deep down something about it didn't seem right. When I close my eyes, I can still see the worn out kitchen linoleum and the water stains on the ceiling and the wallpaper in their mom's house.

• • •

People said my Grandpa George was a hothead and a hell-raiser with a dangerous temper but everybody seemed to like him and listened to what he said, especially when he was giving orders. Louise, the colored woman who worked in the kitchen for us and lived in The Heights, told me she'd seen him throw people out the front door by the seat of their pants, walk them over to the police station next door when they got too loaded, and tell the cop on duty to lock 'em up. I saw him grab hold of a man's hat who tried to cheat him, and pull that thing right down to his shoulders. The guy's head popped through the top like one of those rubber rodents in the whack-a-mole game the carneys set up when they came to town.

My dad also had a hot temper. I knew one thing for sure — you didn't want to cross either one of them and you damn well better pay attention when they talked to you. Everybody else seemed to know that, too.

Life was different in those days. If you fell off your bike or skinned your knee playing football, you'd go home, wash it off with soap and water and put a bandage on it, or just forget about it until dinnertime. If your dad got mad at you, you'd get a leather shoe or a belt across your backside. If you were stupid enough to smart off to your mother or swear out loud, you'd get your mouth washed out with a bar of Lux soap. And if you did something wrong, you were expected to tell the truth and make it right. There wasn't so much gray in the world around us. Ike told me life was about the same at his house, except his dad wasn't around much.

The grown-ups we knew were busy working and doing other stuff so we had to entertain ourselves. On Saturday mornings, we'd watch tag-team wrestling on TV. Sometimes we'd play baseball in the field behind the barn or smoke cigarettes in the old cemetery. When we could, we'd go see Tarzan movies in Hudson, five miles down the road where the rich kids lived. Punishment was when you had to stay home. We didn't even have fences; the yards all ran together.

Every once in a while, Old Man Burridge got behind the wheel of his rusty old Ford flatbed pickup and charged back through the rows in his apple orchard to chase us out of the trees where we spent hours eating his apples and swapping stories about grown-ups. Sometimes when he was mad, he'd stick his shotgun out the front window and fire it in the air to scare us. We'd hit the ground running like jackrabbits through the ryegrass and weeds toward Differt's Pond. Then, we'd double-back to where we'd ditched our bikes and head someplace else to see what we could get away with. Before nightfall, we'd be back in his orchard, eating more apples and throwing apple cores at the side of his barn.

Wally was the most normal person I knew. Grandpa George said he was "the best porter he'd ever known." When I asked him what he meant by "porter," he told me how most of the colored men in the First World War were only allowed to work as porters who carried bags and did chores for the officers.

"The Army had rules against them," he said. "Back in the 1800's, most porters were freed slaves who worked on Pullman railroad cars. Even after they formed a union, they still hardly got paid anything except for tips, maybe two dollars a day for twenty hours of work. Wally's dad came out here from Chicago. Your grandmother and I, we never treated Wally that way. He's a good man. He's done plenty for me and we always paid him fair."

Wally's skin was the color of a Hershey's milk chocolate bar, and his hair was short and gray all over. He always wore a clean flannel shirt and workman's coveralls. I thought he was older than Grandma Moses and Abraham Lincoln put together. He and his daughter, Louise, who ran the kitchen, looked like they moved slow as molasses. But they were always two steps ahead of everyone else. He taught me a lot about what people were supposed to stand for, and most of it had to do with keeping your word, treating people fair, and seeing the good things in life.

Wally always had time for me. We got used to the noise the empty beer bottles made when they came down the chute behind the bar and clanged their way to the basement. It was like living near the railroad tracks or background wallpaper you didn't see anymore. Me and Wally spent a lot of time down there stacking beer and pop cases on the dirt floors — Nehi, Dr Pepper, Coke, and Royal Crown Cola.

I was my grandpa's first-born grandson so he treated me like royalty, at least that's what my sisters said when we were older. They told me they never liked him because he made them feel unimportant. Boys rated higher on the scales back then, just like they do in India and China.

Grandpa George was always trying to toughen me up. "Throw some dirt in their face or stick your finger in their eyes if somebody jumps you and you need to. Go ahead and kick 'em in the balls. That'll stop them."

He took me out in his boat when I spent a summer with him in Arkansas and threw me overboard when I was eleven.

"Swim, Ben. You can do it," he said.

My dad gave me an old photo of Grandpa I pinned up on my bedroom wall. I still have that picture of him wearing his army wool trousers, canvas boot spats, and a dark shirt with two pockets. He's sitting on a chair in the middle of a field getting a shave with a straight edge.

Grandpa George enlisted in the infantry during World War I. He got stationed in England with the Limeys, that's what he called them, and served in France where my dad told me he fought in the trenches. I used to wonder, when I was older, if he'd ever smelled the mustard gas and whether that's why he sometimes had that far off look in his eyes.

When World War II came around, Grandpa George joined the Seabees and went to the South Pacific where he built airstrips and secured the beachheads on islands held by the Japanese. Grandpa waded ashore in the Philippines with MacArthur, whose picture I'd seen in the newsreels and in my history book at school. He gave me some bayonets made from car springs. They had dark, hand-carved wooden handles. I hid the bayonets with a couple of empty fifty millimeter brass shells under my bed where my mother wouldn't see them and kept the door closed when I showed them to my friends. I couldn't tell whether that was dried blood on the blades or something less sinister.

We had one gas pump out in front of the tavern next to the road that ran toward Cleveland. Every once in a while, my dad would ask me to run out and crank the handle under the Sinclair sign with the dinosaur logo. That was when he was giving somebody special treatment or figured they might fill up the tank and take off before paying the bill. Most people knew one another, and the ones who ran businesses, except for a few car mechanics, gave you a fair shake.

When Angelo Cosentino pulled in that day, he was wearing a sharkskin suit and a gray felt hat. He came around every month or so to take the whiskey orders and check on the jukebox racket the mob ran out of Cleveland. I don't know as I'd ever seen someone who looked like he had so much money. It was pouring from his skin and oozing from his pockets. Angelo winked and flipped a fifty-cent piece at me just before he crossed over the wood floor that bucked against the tavern's front door.

When I walked inside a few minutes later, Angelo was sitting at the far end of the bar next to my Grandpa George. There were some Slim Jims and a creepy half-gallon jar of pickled pigs feet in front of them that seemed to mysteriously move around the bar from one customer to another. I never understood why anyone would want to eat something that looked like a disgusting, pink-skinned biology experiment.

My dad stood there with his white apron on, a pencil behind his ear, and a pad of guest checks for the kitchen orders. He took a draw from his El Producto cigar, set it on the edge of the bar, pointed that pencil at Angelo, and wrote it up for a half-pound cheeseburger. He turned around and grabbed the whiskey bottle from the cash register island in back of him, and poured Grandpa and Angelo double-shots. Then he drew two drafts, easy and smooth, like Satchel Paige when he struck out Joe DiMaggio.

Angelo Cosentino wrote on a piece of paper and slid it across the bar to my grandfather who looked back at him, and smiled before he walked over to take a piss in the men's room behind them. I knew every inch of that tavern 'cause I'd cleaned, scrubbed, and painted the place so many times. Whenever my dad asked me to clean that bathroom, I'd talk about homework or tell him I had to help grandma. Squeezing in and out of that place made me think of

The Bible and that saying about a camel going through the eye of a needle. There was barely room for anyone to fit in there next to the urinal with round salt cakes, the toilet bowl behind a double-spring door, and the small mirror with worn, silver spots above the sink. The window was a good fifteen feet above the back parking lot, way too high and narrow even for a scrawny kid like me to climb out.

It was August and hotter than hell that day when my grandpa came back to his customary spot at the bar after doing his bathroom business. We didn't have air conditioning, just a big wood ceiling fan covered with grime and dust that nobody wanted to clean.

Sometimes I worked in the kitchen helping Louise, Wally's daughter. I was glad I wasn't running the fryer or washing dishes that day because I was convinced the extra heat would've made pimples bust through my skin that no amount of Clearasil would cover up. When I looked through the kitchen window, I saw Louise lower a live snapping turtle head first into a big pot of boiling water.

Old Man Henry, who taught me how to hustle pool, had just racked them up and was shooting nine-ball by himself on the table in the back dining room. Mack McLaughlin, and another fellow, were playing a bowling machine game where you slid a metal puck down the wooden alley toward the pins. Those two guys and the regulars seemed like they were always around. The men who worked at the Chrysler plant up the hill would clock-out, run to their cars, drive three miles down to our place, throw down a boilermaker and a sandwich, and be back on the assembly line within thirty minutes. We had to move fast to get things done on time and make money. We were plenty busy, especially around lunchtime and in between shifts.

I don't know what Angelo Cosentino wrote on that paper he passed to my grandfather, but a few minutes later they both walked past the pool table, out the back door, and down the stairs. I trailed behind and watched them from the landing at the top of the tavern's back stairs, the rear entrance customers used. They walked about a hundred feet, around the mud puddles and potholes, down toward the big chestnut tree where Grandpa had parked his two-toned, green and white '54 Lincoln Capri.

That car had every accessory a boy like me could imagine — power steering, power brakes, a deluxe radio with a power antenna, and genuine leather seats that were good enough for the Queen of Sheba. Grandpa George drove as fast as he wanted.

He and Angelo pulled the doors closed and powered the windows all the way up. I figured it had to be at least a hundred and twenty degrees or more inside the Lincoln. The heat was rising off the blacktop's surface in waves, like some kind of midwestern Mojave Desert.

By the time they got out of the car, Angelo's shirt, the one that never had a wrinkle, was soaked clear through. Even so, I thought he still looked pretty cool with his black mustache, fancy hat, and suspenders.

My dad told me that Grandpa had gotten used to the heat during the war. His shirt was still dry, except for a baseball-sized swatch under each arm. He seemed almost super-human to me. They both looked like they were in good spirits.

I walked down the steps and back toward the Lincoln. I could see the beads of sweat on both men's foreheads when they got closer and I caught a whiff of Angelo's Aqua Velva cologne. When I glanced back, I noticed Grandma Cookie watching from the porch of her apartment above the bar. She came down the white wooden steps to the parking lot that sloped away from the back of the tavern toward the chestnut tree. She was smoking a Camel, and holding a highball with ice in her other hand. Grandma walked up to Angelo wearing her long, silk, flowery dress and gave him a big, one-armed hug and a kiss on his cheek. They looked like old, best friends. They talked for a few minutes and laughed together.

Grandpa George and Angelo walked the rest of the way up the slope toward the street that ran in front of the tavern. They were about twenty feet up and to the right from where I was standing, drinking a cola.

Grandpa stopped. They shook hands and Angelo went around to the front of the building where he'd parked. He opened the Cadillac's door, adjusted his rearview mirror, and turned the key.

The explosion was like a sonic boom from a jet, tangled up with metal and glass. The sound pounded inside my head so hard I thought I was deaf.

My grandfather screamed at me. "Get in the basement with Wally. Run goddamn it!"

I could barely hear him.

Within minutes, the fire siren's long, shrill blast wailed through the air. Everybody in town knew what came next because nothing in Twinsburg was more exciting and less routine than that siren. The businessmen who were volunteer firemen ran out of their stores, sometimes leaving their cash registers open. Farmers from miles away climbed off their tractors and ran to their cars. Mechanics rolled out from under and raced to the fire station. Tires screeched and kids wheeled in on their bikes. People ran out of the barbershop three blocks away, and some even came down from The

Heights. It seemed like everybody was there to see those clouds of black smoke shoot up over the roofline.

I looked down and saw Wally standing at the bottom of the steps below me. He motioned for me to come his direction. My heart pounded. Wally started up, grabbed my arm and pulled me over toward the basement steps.

"Stay here with me till we know what's goin' on. If anyone comes round here, you close the door and go get in the coal bin," he said.

My grandma ran up the hill toward where my grandpa was standing. She glanced at me and Wally to make sure we were both okay. I heard her say, "What are we going to do now, George? What if they know this is where the money was going?"

"There's no way they can know," he said. "Angelo hits dozens of places between here and Cleveland." Grandma's shoulders dropped down, and she breathed a sigh of relief.

"Holy hell, Ben, I need to check on Louise and your father. Don't go nowhere," Wally said. He left me and ran toward the basement stairs that led up to the bar and the kitchen. I never saw Wally move as fast as he did that day. He grabbed the wooden stair railing at the other end of the basement away from where I was, and pulled himself up three steps at a time like

Burt Lancaster. I followed and snuck up the stairs about twenty feet behind him.

My dad was behind the bar, smoking a cigar when Wally got to the top. I poked my head out from the basement when Wally ran toward the kitchen. My dad looked worried. How the hell did he keep that cigar lit? If it was me, I figured I would have swallowed it, but taking care of business always came first for him, no matter what. The tavern's front window was shattered in a million pieces. There were shards of glass and sawdust mixed together with the amusement game's bowling pins imbedded in the front wall. One customer had ducked under the bar and still had his hands over his head like they told us to do at school if the Russians bombed us.

Thompson, the Police Chief, and his two deputies ran over from next door and walked around like building inspectors looking for code violations. People started crowding around everywhere. That's when I heard somebody say there were body parts on the curb and by the gas pump. I sneaked out when nobody was looking. There was a pink finger with a big red ruby ring lying all by itself on the sidewalk. I thought about picking it up and putting it under my bed with the empty mortar shells and the bayonets, but that was too gruesome.

Besides, my mother would have beaten the living tar out of me.

Chief Thompson was a big man and more than a little gruff, even on a good day. When he came up to me, later, I got scared. I started thinking about Jimmy Cagney and the candy bar I'd stolen from Kollman's Grocery Store, the one I still hadn't paid for. And then I remembered, how me and Tom Davis had ditched our bikes in the woods near the chief's driveway and put a cherry bomb in his muffler pipe. I thought maybe he was going to arrest me and throw me in a cell with the railroad hobos and what would happen next to me? What are pennies made of? Dirty coppers, I'd tell him, just like Jimmy Cagney said in one of his movies.

"Did you see anything, son?" Chief Thompson said.

"No, sir," I said. "Not a thing. I was in the basement with Wally."

I'd never heard of a car blowing up with a man inside. I imagined Angelo must have looked like a French fry floating around in yesterday's oil, or he was in a million pieces like the window. Funeral parlors and the idea of looking at a dead body, never appealed to me but something made me want to see Angelo's car out front and know what he wrote on that paper and talked with my grandpa about. Chief Thompson never asked me whether I'd seen Mr. Cosentino before, so I kept my mouth shut. I soon found myself remembering how many times he'd carried a canvas duffel bag when he stopped by. And how the three of them, Angelo, Dad and Grandpa, would go down in the basement to talk in the room where they kept the whiskey locked up.

When the fire was out and the cleanup done, Grandpa George and my dad lined up drafts at the bar for all the volunteer firemen. They poured a boilermaker for the chief. And somebody played "Smoke Gets In Your Eyes" on the jukebox. I was happy it still worked. My grandfather had an expression on his face I hadn't ever seen before. He looked worried and detached.

I went back to the kitchen to get myself an ice cold root beer. I opened the refrigerator door and that's when I saw a green duffel bag stuffed full of money on the shelf right next to a stack of T-bone steaks and a pot of turtle soup. Louise pressed her fingers to her lips and made a shhh sound when she saw me open the refrigerator door. I got my pop and left as fast as I could. My mind was racing full speed thinking about all the duffel bags I'd seen Angelo Cosentino carry into the tavern. I knew there was a safe in the floor of the coal bin. Wally and I were the only ones who knew about that safe besides

Dad and Grandpa George. We were under strict orders never to mention it and to always keep it covered up with coal.

The closest I'd ever come to any mob stuff before that day was when Mom and Dad drove us to Chicago to see some of our cousins. We went to a big movie house downtown and then to an Italian restaurant where they baked fresh bread every day and made their own ravioli and pasta. I tried the cannoli. They weren't as good as the old-fashioned, homemade apple pie my mom made.

The kids we met there were all older than me. Their hair was slicked back with pomade and one of them had a switchblade. They all polished their shoes, which I thought was weird, and none of them had ever climbed a tree, so I didn't understand how we could be related.

The only other thing I knew about Italians and Sicily was Short Vincent Street in downtown Cleveland where they had girlie shows and where the mobsters were supposed to hang out. Grandpa George took me there one time and had me wait in the car while he went inside to meet a guy named Big Tony. Afterwards, we went to see the Cleveland Indians and Larry Doby play at the stadium. Then the two of us went down by the waterfront and fished off the pier. I caught two perch, and Grandpa landed a large mouth bass and a sheepshead. We threw them in the cooler in the back of the Lincoln for Louise to cook.

When I think about this stuff now, I realize there were signs they were all on edge before Angelo came. Grandma Cookie smoked more than usual and kept tapping her left foot when we were sitting at the kitchen table, even when there wasn't any music playing. She twisted her cigarettes extra hard when she squashed them in the glass ashtray and kept looking at her watch, asking what day it was.

My grandpa was quieter than usual, and he kept going back to the Lincoln and sitting there alone with the windows rolled up and the hot summer sun beating down. I figured he was thinking about something from the war he didn't want to talk about.

And my dad carried a blackjack nearly all the time, not just when he walked to the bank to make a deposit.

Later that night, Chief Thompson locked up the guy Mrs. Nichols said she saw doing something under Angelo's car when she drove by in her old Plymouth. That night, Grandpa walked down the steps on the side of the police station and went to see the guy in the jail cell who blew up Angelo. The next day I heard the deputy say, "George got close enough to grab hold of him and bust his lip and forehead against the bars. It's a good thing I came in when I did."

When I came to work Tuesday morning, Louise asked me what I thought about what happened. I said I was thankful none of us got blown up. She said she was scared but glad that her father, Wally, was there like a flash of lightning to make sure she and my dad were both okay. She didn't say anything about Grandpa George because everybody figured he was immune from hurt after going through two wars.

When two men dressed in high-priced suits came to post that guy's bail the next day that was big news. Whether it was the fear of God or the fear of my Grandpa George, all I know is, as soon as the guy got out of jail, he walked over, peeled eight, one hundred dollar bills off his roll, and set them on the bar in front of my grandpa. My eyes popped out of my head when I saw that. The deputy told one of the customers, "George told that fella he'd better pay for the damage if he knew what was good for him or he'd take it out of his hide. He warned him not to ever come back." The guy's face was bruised up when I saw him standing next to my grandpa, so I guess he wanted to settle his debt before he left town.

There was supposed to be a hearing or a trial of some kind. Two weeks later, a story appeared on the front page of the *Cleveland Plain Dealer* that said they'd found the guy who murdered

Angelo floating down the Cuyahoga River with a bullet in his head. Somebody important must have been really mad about the guy getting caught, and afraid what he might say. My guess is they didn't think to ask him what he did with the money. They just drilled him.

When I told my friend, C.B., about the incident, he said it was probably the mob. I didn't say anything to him about the money and the duffel bag. People were pretty good about keeping secrets back then, better than now, but I couldn't chance it. And besides, I promised I wouldn't. He told Ike and me we should call the reporter whose name was in the newspaper and ask him who he thought killed the floater. Then we could get the bad guy's picture so if he ever came around, we'd know who to watch out for.

There were plenty of places to hide from the mob and I knew the fastest way to get to all of them. Besides Old Man Burridge's orchard, we had a tree house in Trent Ford's backyard. The old cemetery where we went to smoke and the big sewer pipe that ran down from the elementary school, under the street, and over near where the Dairy Queen was. Then there was the coatroom trap door in the Grange Hall that connected to an old tunnel. And the caves in the woods behind my other grandparent's house where we swung on monkey vines, the overlook near where the hobos camped, and the fake wall in Dodson's house where slaves were hidden during the Civil War.

Of course, we could also go up to The Heights, where Wally, Louise, Ike and Ada lived. I'd never seen any Italians wearing suits in that neighborhood. There were three or four hundred small houses there, most of them made of clapboard and tarpaper. Mordecai Jones had the only one made of brick. Sometimes when I rode past it on my bike, I thought about the story of the three little pigs and the big bad wolf. I guess that's because Mordecai's house seemed stronger and better protected than the other ones.

I guess that's when it first occurred to me what to do with the money in that bag. I thought about it off and on for the better part of a week, and the idea just kept coming back like a cricket hopping on and off my sleeping bag.

I never had a clue until the day the car blew up that my family was helping Angelo Cosentino stash the money he ripped off from the mob. I knew the money was in the coal bin. If nobody was using it, what exactly would be the harm in spreading it around? I could get Ike some new shoes and that dress Ada liked so much in the dress shop window when we saw it. She was pretty nice for a girl.

The combination to the safe was etched on a

stone even with the floor in back of where we stacked the beer and pop cases. I waited till Wally had gone home. Then, I put my fingers on the safe's lock and turned to five, then eight, then forty-five, the day World War II ended in Europe. I stuffed some bundles of twenty-dollar bills from the safe into my newspaper bag and strapped the bag to my bike. If the mob's money was in the safe, then I figured it was already stolen. I'd just be delivering it to a better place, like Robin Hood did in olden times. Otherwise, they probably would have spent it on pomade, cannoli, strippers, and who knows what else.

As far as I knew, they didn't have a police department in The Heights, so I didn't have to worry about that and Chief Thompson spent all his time "protecting and serving" the white folks in town. The tavern was just one stop on Angelo's delivery and collection route.

I pedaled up the hill to the Baptist Church where Wally was a deacon, went through the side door, and put the money inside the sanctuary right below the pulpit. I couldn't stop smiling when I imagined Ike and so many other black kids wearing new shoes and clothes the next week at school, and how happy Ada would be when she saw herself in the mirror.

Wally later told me how the preacher said the money was a gift everyone should be grateful for. I never told Wally what I did, but I think he figured it out. He and my grandpa went way back. There was something between them they never talked about.

My dad was the first to discover the money was missing. I heard him cursing and empty cigar boxes getting slammed against the coal bin's black wall. I was scared when he called me. "Ben," he said, "get in here, right now."

I was out back in the parking lot sitting on the steps that went up to my grandpa's place.

"What the hell happened to the money that was in here? You took some of it, didn't you?" He stuffed a cigar back in his mouth and stared at me, waiting for an answer.

I didn't say anything.

Grandpa came in a minute or two later. "What's going on? What's all the ruckus?" He looked at my dad and then turned toward me. The door to the safe was open. The pile wasn't as high as it had been.

"Ben, what did you do?"

I felt myself grow taller, calmer. I wasn't afraid anymore. "I took some of it," I said. "I took it up to The Heights, to the Baptist Church. I didn't tell anybody."

"You can't do stuff like that," my dad said. "It wasn't your money. This is grown-up business you're messing with."

I could see how pissed he was. I'd gotten a

belt across my backside and been grounded for less. Much less.

My grandpa turned to me. “What made you think you could do that, Ben?”

“I did what I thought was right, same as you, Grandpa when you went to war.”

“What’s that supposed to mean?” my dad said.

That’s when I said, “Hitler was crazy. He wanted to rule the world. He was the worst kind of bully. Grandpa went to war to stop him. He didn’t say it was somebody else’s problem and he couldn’t do anything about it. And you enlisted too, Dad.”

“That was war,” my grandpa declared.

“But you did what you thought was right,” I said.

“You took money that didn’t belong to you, Ben,” my dad said.

“What about the money you guys got from Angelo?”

“That’s different,” my dad said. “We did it because we needed it. We’ve got houses and kids and families to support. And besides, it was the mob’s money.”

“That’s the same thing I figured. Those mob guys weren’t going to do anything good with that money and we’ve got enough compared to Ike and Wally and Louise and the people in The Heights.” I paused for a moment to catch up with myself and what was going through my mind. "They're part of my family, too."

They exchanged glances with each other.

"Wally told me how you got jumped and four guys were beating the living tar out of you, Grandpa, until he stepped in and pulled them off. You and Wally weren't blood-related but that didn't matter 'cause he was your friend. You knew you could count on him."

"Wally told you about that?" Grandpa George said. He looked surprised, and winked at me.

"It's the same for my friends and me. I've got way more than what I need, and Ike's got cardboard that sticks out of his shoes when he walks in the snow. I don't need an invitation or a trophy or somebody to tell me it's okay to do what's right. Those gangsters can go to hell as far as I'm concerned." I kicked a piece of coal against the basement wall.

"I just wanted to balance the scales. There's no good reason for things to stay the same just because they always have been."

"Why did you give it to the preacher?" Grandpa said.

"I knew he wouldn't keep it for himself. I knew he'd spread it around, and I'm happy I did. I don't feel guilty. I stood up for something."

Both of them stared at me for what seemed like a long time. And then they grinned. I felt like I'd hit a home run in the last of the ninth they both got to see. I suppose it was dangerous and naïve, but my Grandpa George, like Louise said, had already been through two wars, so I figured he and my dad could handle just about anything life could throw at them.

"Grandpa, you always told me when a chance like this comes around, a chance to make a difference, I should grab it. And that if it didn't come around, I'd better get up off my butt and go look for it. Well, that's what I did."

Like the book? Tell your friends. Circulate the word on social media and via book clubs, so the story isn't lost. Post a review. I'd appreciate hearing from you. Here's how to post one on Amazon:

Go to the detail page for the item on Amazon.com.

Click "write a customer review" in the Customer Reviews section.

Rate the book and write your review. Click submit.

The author is available for select readings, including book clubs when possible. To inquire about a possible appearance, please contact **Daniel@AuthorDanielBabka.com**

ABOUT THE AUTHOR

Daniel Babka grew up in a small midwestern town like the one described in this story. He served in VISTA, the domestic Peace Corps, attended law school and a theological seminary, managed housing in New York City's toughest neighborhoods, and ran a couple of small, start-up companies. He's an avid hiker who, like Dylan Blake, the detective he writes about in *No More Illusions* and *Dirt Crappis,* needs time in the woods.

Daniel has two grown children and lives in the Northern California foothills. He's a member of the California Writers Club and a small writer's critique group. He is presently finishing work on his second Dylan Blake novel, *Dirt Crappis,* and several more short stories.

ALSO BY DANIEL BABKA

***No More Illusions. . . A Mystery*:** Dylan Blake has had some losses in his life — a brother who committed suicide, a father killed by a drunk driver, a marriage that didn't work. The scars have stayed with him. A rookie cop at age 41, promoted to Detective 1st Grade after 18 months, Blake unexpectedly finds his vacation interrupted when the Chief of Police calls and asks him to take a look at an accident scene along the Pacific Coast Highway near Big Sur. Blake's discovery pulls him back to his own painful memories and sets a chain of events in motion that unearth a family's secrets about murder and the way morality can be made to bend.

***Two States and A Thousand Miles*:** a short, slice-of-life story about two people whose lives intersect in a profound way.

***Dirt Crappis*:** a second Dylan Blake novel, soon to be published.

for mature audiences
PREVIEW FOLLOWS. . .

"Hard-core reality is, there are plenty of people, selfish people who want what they want and who pretend not to see the bodies in the street when they drive over them. It's just like what John Lewis, the Georgia congressman who marched with Dr. King and the Freedom Riders, said: 'You've got to put yourself in the way of what's wrong, find the courage to get in trouble, good trouble, necessary trouble.'"

"I don't much care what the consequences are," Blake said. "I like what I do, but I had a job before I became a detective and I'll have one afterwards."

BEFORE

Kathryn Winslow picked up Jack Hamilton's personal belongings, the easy-to-grab stuff, and dropped them in a banker's box. She carried it through the middle of an office full of employees sitting at their desks on both sides of the room. Then, she put the box on the sidewalk out front, still wet from a short summer rain, before walking back to the desk where Hamilton stood. He didn't say a word.

"You've got thirty minutes to get the rest of your stuff and get out," Kathryn said. Her lips trembled for a moment.

He could feel the color drain from his face. His stomach knotted up. His hands began to shake. "You can't be serious. This is crazy. I've invested twelve years of my life building this business with you from the ground up. We're partners. What the hell do you think you're doing, Kathryn?"

"I'm calling a locksmith," she said.

Hamilton was stunned.

"Thirty minutes, no more. You can sue me if you want. I don't care. It's over."

• • •

He felt betrayed. Kathryn Winslow was his closest friend. He'd played that day over and over in his mind for the last six months, searching for an answer that made sense, that would bring him closure. He didn't see the end coming. The business was going to be the legacy he left to his children, his retirement nest egg, and it was gone.

Kathryn Winslow had lied. She'd promised him half. He'd spent days staring at the ceiling, waiting for the phone to ring, expecting her to call and tell him she'd made a mistake. The lawsuit, the break-in, a real sense that someone had been watching him, the revolver in his glove box. All of it was out of sync with the way his life used to be.

His mind drifted with the fog across the highway. The vintage Jaguar picked up speed on the downhill side. The tires squealed when Hamilton rounded the first curve. The second turn came sooner than he expected. A line of three cars headed north on the other side of the double-yellow line facing him. He eased off the accelerator, and hit the brake. His palms began to sweat. He gripped the steering wheel harder. Then his knuckles turned white.

Hamilton's car crossed over the pavement, ran over the weeds, and ripped through the guard rail. The car sailed over the cliff along the coast highway like a baseball arcing over the center field fence, before it began to fall like a dead weight. He looked up at his rearview mirror for a long second and saw the mountains behind him before the rocks crashed through the windshield. The sea's foam swirled around him, and took his breath away.

CHAPTER ONE

Dylan Blake left the campground in Big Sur with no agenda in mind beyond letting the day unfold. He'd spent five days relaxing, swimming in the ocean, sleeping under the stars, and hiking. It centered him, the same way a Zen garden did other people. A condor, riding the wind currents along the coast near Garrapata, soared over his head the day before. And he'd seen another in the canyons below the Carmel Highlands near the cloud lines that stretched across the Pacific.

The sound of the Audi's turbo running through the gears and accelerating along Highway One, interrupted his thoughts. The car held the road and cornered with a surge of power that went straight to his head like a shot of good tequila. Blake turned his cell phone on and set it between the Audi's seats, then put in a CD.

Ten minutes later, the phone rang. Chief Cooper's name appeared on the blue dashboard display. The Rolling Stones went silent. Blake hesitated for a moment, knowing he'd be back on the clock as soon as he answered. He hadn't taken a real vacation for two years. Except for the chief's invitation to join the force, Cooper had never called him.

"I was hoping you'd check on something for me if you're still around the coast, Blake."

"Give me a minute to pull over, Chief."

Cooper's voice was as unmistakable as Spencer Tracy's. Blake had been on the police force close to four years. He wasn't naive, but when he heard guys like Cooper, he was inclined to believe what they said and do what they asked.

Blake's mother told him his dad could sell ice to the Eskimos. He figured Cooper had that same kind of James Garner, Rockford Files talent. Blake angled toward the dirt road off Highway One that ran down toward Partington Cove where mules pulled sleds loaded with tanbark oak down to the water's edge at the turn of the century, and liquor was smuggled during Prohibition. The black Audi sport coupe's tires crunched to a stop against the gravel. Blake left the engine running so the turbo could cool down, and reached for the black leather note pad on the seat beside him.

"I'll bet that water is cold as ever down there," Cooper said. "You probably thought you'd be surfing when you moved out here from the mid-west. Didn't know you'd need a wetsuit if you didn't want to freeze your nuts off."

"Yeah, you're right," Blake said. He rolled down the car's back windows, cut off the engine, got out to stretch his legs. "Go ahead, tell me what you need, Chief."

"I know somebody here in Sierra Springs, a friend of the department, whose business partner went missing a few days ago. She tells me he's turned up at the bottom of a cliff next to the coast highway. I'd like you to take a look, then check in with the local sheriff and see what he's thinking. The guy's apartment here in Sierra Springs was broken into last week and some business records are missing. His partner is suspicious."

"What's his name?" Blake said.

"Jack Hamilton. The car's somewhere south of Big Sur on the way to the sheriff's sub-station. I know the sheriff down there . . . Kowalski. I'll let him know you're coming. He and I go back a ways."

Kowalski, Blake scribbled. He underlined it twice and drew a circle around the name. "I'll have to check it out tomorrow morning. I'm too far away right now."

"Take a look at the accident scene. Whatever you see, keep it to yourself for now. Take an extra day or two. The department will cover your expenses and I'll clear your schedule. Have you caught any fish?"

"Didn't bring a pole," Blake said. "I don't do much fishing. I didn't plan on catching anything before your call, besides a suntan."

"That might change. You're on the clock now. I'll see you when you get back."

The last thing Blake wanted was to get caught in the middle of something between Cooper and a sheriff he didn't know in another jurisdiction. Blake pulled into a bait shop on his way to Big Sur, bought a Dr. Pepper and a chart that forecasted the tide levels.

He drove through town to the Henry Miller Memorial Library on the other side of Nepenthe where he could use an internet connection to email his girlfriend, Julianna.

He felt good about his life, close to certain he wouldn't find any other detectives reading D.H. Lawrence's poetry. He picked a copy of *The Tropic of Cancer* and flipped through the pages.

"I have no money, no resources, no hopes. I am the happiest man alive," Henry Miller wrote.

Blake had never pictured himself settling for everyday routine. He'd walked away from law school after his second year — too much paperwork, not enough action. He figured police work had to be more exciting than sitting behind a desk, reading case law and looking for legal precedents.

Twenty years earlier he'd stopped at that library with his ex-wife. Those were the days when he confused Henry Miller with Arthur Miller, an error he now attributed to his public school education and a fragmentary recollection obscured by smoking too much weed. Back then, he didn't know who Anais Nin, Henry Miller's lover, was. Now Blake's beat generation friend, Edison, at 24-Hour Fitness, was telling him stories about the week he and Nin spent together in Paris during the '60s.

The tall cross some artist had fashioned from computer monitors, was still standing guard in the museum's redwood grove. The ambiance, the books, live music under the stars —all of it was still happening. Henry Miller's library was a shrine more suited to intellectuals and free spirits than police detectives.

He'd been staying in a campground in Big Sur. The land kept him connected to the parts of himself he valued most, the ones that began to slip away when he got distanced from the mountains and the woods. He'd picked out a spot about thirty-feet from where the creek ran through the redwoods. He sacked out around ten and set his alarm for the ungodly hour of 2:45 a.m., so he could catch the low tide in the morning and escape attention from passers-by and the local authorities. It didn't take long before the sound of running water pulled him up like a magnet to pee in the middle of the night, just like it had the first five nights he'd been there. He looked up at the moon's midnight glow and a sky filled with stars that filtered through the tent's screen windows above his head.

The alarm clock broke into his dream. Blake grabbed some power bars and raw almonds, rolled up his sleeping bag, quietly pulled out of the campground, and headed south down Highway One toward San Louis Obispo. The road was close to deserted. He needed coffee but didn't have any. Sunrise was still a good two hours away. He turned up the car's CD player and listened to R&B and acid jazz to keep alert.

The mile marker on Highway One Chief Cooper had given him came into view. He slowed down and pulled to the side when he saw the yellow caution tape and sawhorses by the curve. The sun had begun to break. He got out and walked to the edge of the cliff where the coastal scrub trees and chaparral grew.

The car was silver gray, like Cooper said, an older vintage Jag, laying about three hundred feet below. There were no brake marks. The bumper arched upward, nested between the rocks, the kelp, and the water. A new day was rolling across the Pacific and the morning fog had begun to lift as the sun inched up the hills. The chill in the salt air wrapped itself around him.

"How the hell is anyone ever going to get that thing back up here?" Blake mumbled, when he saw the Jag. Search and rescue must have lowered somebody down in a sling to bring the body up. Either that or a helicopter.

The descent was obviously too dangerous from where he was, so Blake drove to the next turn-off. His hiking boots and poles, and the climbing rope he'd used in Utah when he ventured into some slot canyons, were in his trunk. He got his gear out, including a hydration pack and his binoculars, and scrambled over some rocks and scrub brush for a better look. He decided to rappel down. His legs were still fatigued from fourteen miles of hiking the day before.

He took his time to reach the water where Hamilton's body had lain motionless two days earlier, next to the tide pool full of hermit crabs, anemones, and starfish. The water was cold and crystal clear, with big jellyfish that looked like eggs over easy on steroids submerged in the water about twenty feet out. The long, tubular strands of kelp reached for the shore.

Blake set his backpack and gear on the rocks

that were safe from the tide, and moved closer. He spotted a small shred of Hamilton's shirt mangled in with the metal and blood spattered on the car's steering wheel and dash. He dabbed his handkerchief where the blood was thickest, put it in a plastic zip-lock bag, and stuffed it in his shirt pocket. Then he forced open the glove compartment and found it empty. No doubt the local police had already bagged and emptied the contents. The sedan's back doors had been jammed shut by the impact. Blake climbed in through the front door window. He figured the car had been swept clean, that is, until he found a one-way airline ticket from L.A. to Playa del Carmen, the Mexican Riviera, stuffed inside a soggy newspaper behind the driver's seat.

The sun had begun to edge higher up the slopes of the Santa Lucia Mountains beyond the cliff's edge that towered above him. Blake climbed back out the driver's window, moved around to the back of the car, and pried open the trunk. Empty. He looked closely to make sure the car was steady and wouldn't shift, then crawled underneath to check the brakes and steering. Left front, right rear—the brake lines had clearly been loosened. Blake saw the markings and the fluid, and photographed them. He took a shot of the car's front end and another of the license plate. This is enough, he thought to himself. I need to get out of here.

Blake looked around with his binoculars. No one was in sight. Twenty minutes later, as he balanced his weight and climbed up the most difficult part of the trail open to view, he heard the rocks falling. Small ones slipped past him at first and then there was a thunderous downpour of dirt. He felt the earth shake. He swung back, grabbed the smooth hard root of a Madrone tree and pulled himself under a shallow overhang where the earth had fallen away. He kept his body as straight as he could, one foot jammed against a rock, the other dangling in the air. He stayed there for several minutes. The first rock tumbled down hard, a foot from his head, and smashed into Hamilton's car. "Holy shit!" he said.

Blake caught his breath, steadied himself, and waited before he began to inch his way out. He felt his heart pounding against his chest.

He reached for the binoculars on his belt as soon as he got to a ledge twenty-feet higher that felt safe. He dug his fingers into the grass and scrub for a grip, clawed, and pushed hard with his boot heels against the rock outcrops buried in the cliff's face. His head and chest were exposed and vulnerable, back and arms wet with sweat. Blake kept looking up. He didn't hear anything except the crash of the surf below. He saw a gradual slope to the right with a vein in the rock facing that looked safe. He moved across some lose patches of rock and the brush that was anchored in, zigzagging one step at a time. Blake skidded on a small avalanche of gravel, righted himself and continued to crawl up until he reached the vein. He followed it up to the rim and pressed his chest against the earth, relieved, when he got near the top.

Fifty minutes had gone by. The road was clear in both directions. He stood, walked to his car, stuffed his gear in the trunk and stashed the camera in the wheel-well next to the spare tire. Blake knelt down and looked at the Audi's underside before he headed south. He'd been a cop long enough to know the consequences attached to being careless or over-confident.

Blake braked a couple times before he picked up speed, with an eye on his rear view mirror. When he got back to the area the police had roped off, he got out to take a second look. He spotted some fresh boot prints in the mud near the berm and scratch marks near the bottom of two large rocks anchored near the edge of the cliff on the other side of the guard rail. Mother nature didn't make marks like that. Somebody with a pry bar had.

15672356R00037

Made in the USA
Middletown, DE
15 November 2014